Puppy In my Pocket

Trick or Treat

SCHOLASTIC READER
LEVEL 3
700-1500 WORDS

By Sierra Harimann
Illustrated by The Artifact Group

SCHOLASTIC INC.

New York   Toronto   London   Auckland

Sydney   Mexico City   New Delhi   Hong Kong

ISBN 978-0-545-28144-7

© 2011 MEG. All Rights Reserved.

PUPPY IN MY POCKET® and all related titles, logos, and characters are registered trademarks of MEG.
Licensed by Licensing Works!®

Published by Scholastic Inc. SCHOLASTIC and associated logos are trademarks and/or
registered trademarks of Scholastic Inc.
Lexile is a registered trademark of MetaMetrics, Inc.

12 11 10 9 8 7 6 5 4 3 2 1   11 12 13 14 15 16/0

Designed by Angela Jun
Printed in the U.S.A.
First printing, September 2011   40

It was almost Halloween, and Fuji was excited to go trick-or-treating. But first she needed to think of the perfect costume to wear.

"Do you know what costume you're going to wear for Halloween?" Fuji asked her friend Ivy.

"Of course!" Ivy said. "I am going to dress like a queen. What else would I be?"

"How about you, Clarissa?" Fuji asked.
"I'm going to dress like a fairy," Clarissa barked. "I'll wear shimmery wings and a flower crown."

The doorbell rang and Fuji ran to the front door. It was her friend Ora.

"Hi, Fuji," Ora barked. "I want to invite you and your friends to a costume ball at Masquerade Mansion. I designed the invitations myself."

Ora gave Fuji a pretty envelope.

"Thanks, Ora," Fuji told her friend. "That sounds like fun."

Gigi entered the room. "Ooh, la la," she said. "A fancy costume ball? I'm going to dress as a ballerina. I'll wear a pink tutu and a sparkling tiara."

"See you there!" Ora said as she waved good-bye.

"Your ballerina costume sounds special," Fuji told Gigi. "I still need to think of the perfect thing to wear. And now it will have to work for trick-or-treating *and* the ball."

"You could dress up as a cowgirl," Clarissa suggested.

"That would be fun," Fuji said. "But I'm not sure that's the right costume for me."

"Well, you could be a mummy or a ghost," Ivy offered. But Fuji shook her head. "Too scary!"

Spike and Freddy bounded into the room. They were wearing matching eye patches.

"Ahoy, mateys," Spike barked. "Freddy and I are going to be pirates for Halloween."

"Shiver me timbers!" Freddy growled playfully.

"Fuji, you can be a pirate, too," Gigi suggested.
"I'm not sure I'd be a good pirate," Fuji said sadly.
"I'm not good at growling."

"I have an idea," Clarissa said. "Let's go to the costum
shop. Maybe Fuji will find something to wear there."
"Okay," Fuji agreed. "Let's do it!"

10

"This will be *grrrrreat*," said Spike in his pirate accent. "Maybe I can find a paw hook at the costume shop."

"And I still need a tutu," Gigi said.

The puppies tried on lots of costumes.

"What do you think of these fairy wings?" Clarissa asked.

"*Très chic!*" Gigi said. "That means *very stylish* in French."

"What do you think of that baseball player costume?" Gigi asked Fuji.

"I don't know," Fuji replied. "It's fun, but I just don't think it's right for me. I want a costume that's exciting. I would love to wear a mask to the ball."

The costume shop was closing for the night, so the puppies had to decide what to buy quickly.

"I just love my velvet cape!" Ivy told her friends. "It's so regal."

"*Garr!*" Spike growled as he waved his new shiny hook at Freddy. "You'll be walking the plank, Captain!"

"Did you find a costume you liked, Fuji?" Clarissa asked. But Fuji just shook her head sadly.

"Cheer up, Fuji!" Freddy said. "We still have a few days until the costume ball. I'm sure you'll think of something."

The puppies headed back toward Puppyville Manor.

Suddenly, Fuji heard a soft crying sound.

"Shh!" she barked at her friends. "Did you hear that?"

Clarissa nodded. "It sounds like someone is in trouble."

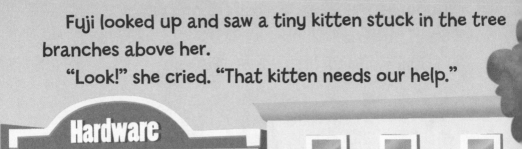

Fuji looked up and saw a tiny kitten stuck in the tree branches above her.

"Look!" she cried. "That kitten needs our help."

Freddy tried to reach up to offer the kitten a paw, but the branch was too high.

"I'm supposed to be a fierce pirate, but this hook isn't much help," Spike admitted.

Fuji looked around her. Suddenly, she had an idea. "I know what to do," she told her friends. "Let's borrow a ladder from the hardware store. We can use it to get the kitten out of the tree."

"That's a great idea," Clarissa said. "Let's go!"
Together, the puppies carried the ladder from the
store to the tree. They propped up the ladder so that
Fuji could climb up to reach the kitten.

Fuji spoke softly to the frightened kitten. "It's okay," she said. "I'm here to help. Just climb on my back, and I'll get you down from this branch."

When Fuji reached the bottom of the ladder, the other puppies cheered.

"Fuji, you're a hero," Freddy barked.

The kitten kissed her on the ear.

Fuji blushed.

"Thanks, Freddy, but I'm no hero," Fuji said modestly. "I just did the same thing you would have done if you had the idea. But you just gave me an amazing idea for a Halloween costume."

"I'm going to be a superhero!" Fuji said happily.

"That's a *grrrrreat* idea," Spike said.

"Oui, oui!" Gigi cried. "That's how we say *yes* in French!"

Before the puppies knew it, Halloween arrived.
They dressed up in their costumes and went
trick-or-treating all afternoon.

As soon as the sun began to set, the puppies made their way to Masquerade Mansion for the costume ball.

Ora greeted her friends at the door.
"Welcome to Masquerade Mansion!" she said.
The chef, Dougie, offered the puppies special treats
he had made.

Ora introduced everyone to her friend Honey.
"Nice to meet y'all," Honey said in a Southern
accent. "You're just in time for the costume parade!"

"A parade?" Freddy asked. "Wow! This is the best party ever."

"I couldn't agree more," Fuji barked happily. "Happy Halloween, everyone!"